Stiff Upper Lip

STIFF UPPER LIP

by

Lawrence Durrell

Nicolas Bentley drew the pictures

FABER AND FABER
London

First published in 1958
by Faber and Faber Limited
*3 Queen Square London WC*1
First published in this edition 1966
Reprinted 1968, 1971 *and* 1976
Printed in Great Britain by
Whitstable Litho Ltd Whitstable Kent
All rights reserved
© *Lawrence George Durrell*
1958

ISBN 0 571 06722 0

Acknowledgements
to the Editors of:
Lilliput for *La Valise*
the *New Statesman* for *Cry Wolf*
and the *Sunday Times* for *Stiff Upper Lip*,
Something à la Carte?, *The Unspeakable
Attaché*, *The Game's the Thing*, *If Garlic
be the Food of Love*, *Where the Bee Sucks*
and *The Iron Hand*

Contents

. . . une petite splendeur

Stiff Upper Lip

As for the Fair Sex (said Antrobus), I am no expert, old boy. I've always steered clear. Mind you, I've admired through binoculars as one might admire a fine pair of antlers. Nearest I ever came to being enmeshed was in the *Folies Bergères* one night. Fortunately, Sidney Trampelvis was there and got me out into the night air and fanned me with his cape until my head cleared and I realized the Full Enormity of what I'd done. Without realizing it, I had proposed to a delightful little pair of antlers called Fifi and was proposing to take her back to the Embassy and force the Chaplain to gum us up together. Phew! I certainly owe Sidney a debt. We positively galloped away from the place in a horse-drawn contrivance with our opera hats crushed like puff-pastry. Sidney, who was only visiting, and who had also crossed the subliminal threshold and proposed—dear God—to a contortionist; Sidney was even paler than I. That night he dyed his hair green to escape identification and crossed over to Dover on the dusk packet—a bundle of nerves.

But Dovebasket in love was a strange sight. His sighs echoed through the Chancery. There were sonnets and triolets and things all over the backs of the War Office despatches. The little winged youth had certainly pinked him through the spencer. Yes, it was Angela, Polk-Mowbray's niece. I can't think why Polk-Mowbray didn't liquidate one or both of them. But then the Popular Verdict on *him* was that he needed stiffening. Yes, the stiffest thing about him was perhaps his upper lip. As for Dovebasket, I would have described him as an ensanguined poop. A spoon, my dear chap, a mere spoon. Yet love makes no distinctions. Afterwards he published a little book of his poems called *Love Songs of an Assistant Military Attaché* with a preface by Havelock Ellis. A rum book in sooth. I remember one refrain:

> *The moon gleams up there like a cuspidor*
> *Angela, Angela, what are we waiting for?*

You get the sort of stuff? Could lead directly to Nudism. It was clear from all this that he was terribly oversexed and I for one felt that he would end in Botany Bay or the Conservative Central Office or somewhere. You see, Angela wouldn't respond to the rowel at all. Not her. Press his suit as firmly as he might the wretched chap only got the tip-tilted nose in response. It was clear that she considered him as no more than a worm-powder. And here I must add that we had all been worried about Angela, for she had been showing signs of getting one of her famous crushes on the Russian Military Attaché— Serge, or Tweed, or something by name—a bloater to boot. But of course, the worst aspect of it all was that we weren't officially fraternizing at that time with The Other Bloc. Polk-Mowbray was worried about her security. He had been frightfully alarmed to overhear an idle conversation of hers with a Pole in which she gave away—without a moment's thought—the entire lay-out of Henley Regatta, every disposition, old boy. She even drew a map of the refreshment room. I know that Henley isn't Top Secret, but it might just as easily have been the dispositions of the Home Fleet. Such lightness of speech argued ill for the Mission. One simply did not know what she mightn't reveal in this way. . . . We were concerned, I might say, Quite Concerned.

Well, it so fell out that during this fruitless romance of Dovebasket's the Vulgarians invited us all to join them in pushing out the boat for the Wine Industry. They had always had a Wine Industry, mind you, but it had never been put on a proper basis before. So, very wisely, they had imported a trio of French experts and turned them loose among the bins. Within a matter of a couple of years, the whole thing had been reorganized, new cultures had been sorted out, and Vulgaria was now about to launch about twenty new wines upon the export market. Advance intelligence from old Baron Hisse la Juppe, the Military Attaché (who had practically lived down there while experiments were going on) suggested that something most promising had taken place. Vulgaria, he said (rather precariously) was on the point of exporting wines which would equal anything the French and Italians could do. . . . We were incredulous, of course, but were glad to assist in the send-off of the new wines. The whole Corps accepted the invitation to the *Vin d'Honneur* with alacrity.

The day dawned bright and fair, and it was a merry party of carefree dips who took the train north to the vineyards. The whole *vieillesse dorée* of diplomacy, old man.

In sparkling trim. For once, the whole thing was admirably worked out; we were carried in vine-wreathed carriages to the great main cellars of the place—more like a railway tunnel than anything, where warm candle-light glowed upon twinkling glasses and white linen; where the music of minstrels sounded among the banks of flowers. . . . I must say, I was transported by the beauty of the scene. There lay the banks of labelled bottles, snoozing softly upon the trestles with the candles shining upon their new names. Our hosts made speeches. We cheered. Then corks began to pop and the wine-tasting began. One of the French specialists led us round. He tried to get us to take the thing rather too professionally—you know, shuffling it about in the mouth, cocking the chin up to the ceiling and then spitting out into a kind of stone draining-board. Well as you know, one is trained to do most things in the F.O. But not to spit out good wine. No. We simply wouldn't demean ourselves by this niggardly shuffling and spitting out. We swallowed. I think you would have done the same in our place. What we were given to taste, we tasted. But we put the stuff away.

And what stuff, my dear boy. Everything that Hisse la Juppe had said proved true. What wines! Wines to set dimples in the cheeks of the soul. Some were little demure white wines, skirts lifted just above the knee, as it were. Others just showed an elbow or an ankle. Others were as the flash of a nymph's thigh in the bracken. Wines in sables, wines in mink! What an achievement for the French! Some of the range of reds struck out all the deep bass organ-notes of passions—in cultured souls like ours. It was ripping. We expanded. We beamed. Life seemed awfully jolly all of a sudden. We rained congratulations upon our hosts as we gradually wound along the great cellars, tasting and judging. What wines! I couldn't decide for myself, but after many trials fell upon a red wine with a very good nose. You see, we each had to pick one, as a free crate of it was to be given to each member of the Corps. Sort of Advertisement.

And as we went along the French specialist enchanted us by reading out from his card the descriptions of the wines which we were trying. What poetry! I must hand it to the French, though they tend to make me suspicious in lots of ways. There was one, for example, a sort of hock, which was described as *"au fruité parfait, mais présentant encore une légère pointe de verdeur nullement désagréable.* Another was described as *"séveux et bien charpenté"*. And then there was a sort of Vulgarian Meursault which was *"parfait de noblesse et de finesse, une petite splendeur."* I must say, for a moment one almost succumbed to culture, old man. The stuff was damned good. Soon we were all as merry as tom-tits, and I even smiled by mistake at the Bulgarian Chargé. In fact everything would have gone off like a dream if Dovebasket hadn't cut up rough and sat deliberately on the air-conditioning.

Apparently in the middle of all this bonhomie the wretched youth crept up on Angela and breathed a winged word in her ear. It was the old fateful pattern. She turned on her heel and tossing up her little chin went over to the other corner where the crapulous Serge was swigging the least significant of the wines with much smacking of the lips. It was so obvious; Dovebasket was cut as if by a whiplash. A cry of fury broke from his lips to find that she preferred this revolting foreigner who had apparently been named after an inferior British export material; he banged his fist upon the nearest table and cried out, "If I cannot have her, nobody shall!" And all of a sudden made his way to the corner of the tunnel of love and sat down. He took a copy of Palgrave's Golden Brewery from his pocket—one of those anthologies with a monotonous-looking cover—and started to read in a huffy way. Sulks, old man, mortal sulks.

Well, we sighed and went on with our bibbing, unaware that the fellow was sitting upon our life-line, as it were. I have already said that he was mechanically-minded. Apparently he had noticed that the air-supply to the tunnel came through a sort of sprocket with a side-valve cut in a sort of gasket with a remote-control intake —how does one say these things? Anyway. Dovebasket placed his behind firmly on the air-screw, thus cutting off our oxygen supply from the outer world. It was all very well trying to suffocate his rival. But—and such is the power of passion—he was determined to suffocate the entire Corps.

Well, for ages nobody noticed anything. On we went from cask to cask, in ever-growing merriment, getting more and more courtly, with each swig. We thought that Dovebasket was just alone and palely loitering, that he would grow out of it. We didn't know that he was sitting on the very H_2SO_4 or H_2O (I never was much good at chemistry) which nourished human life in these regions. I had never thought much about air before. Apparently there is something quite essential about it. Nutritious as wine is, it cannot apparently sustain life unaided. Well, as I say, there we were unaware of the formaldehyde bubbles which were slowly crawling up the bloodstream, mounting to our brains. Suddenly I noticed that everyone seemed unwontedly hilarious, a rather ghastly sort of hilarity, mind you. Laughter, talk, music—it all seemed to have gone into a new focus.

STIFF UPPER LIP

A grimly bacchanalian note set in. I was vaguely aware that things were not as they should be but I couldn't quite put my finger on it. The first to go was Gool, the British Council man. He lay down quietly in a bed of roses and passed out, only pausing to observe that he could feel the flowers growing over him. We ignored him. The music had got rather ragged at the edges. People were drinking on rather desperately now and talking louder than ever. Somewhere in the heart of it all there was a Marked Discomfort. People seemed suddenly to have aged, bent up. You could begin to see how they would look at ninety if they lived that long. The chiefs of mission had gone an ashen colour. As if they had worn their expressions almost down to the lining. It is hardly believable what a difference air can make to dips, old man.

And now it was that knees began to buckle, stays to creak, guy-ropes to give. Still, in courtly fashion, people began to look around them for something to lean on. Yes, people everywhere began to strap-hang, still talking and laughing, but somehow in a precarious way. Polk-Mow-bray had gone a distinctly chalky colour and had difficulty in articulating; the Argentine Minister had quite frankly started to crawl towards the entrance on all fours.

It was Serge, I think, who first noticed the cause of our plight. With a bound he was at Dovebasket's side crying, "Please to remove posterior from the breathing," in quite good Satellite English. Dovebasket declined to do so. Serge pulled him and received a knee in the chest. Dovebasket settled himself firmly once more and showed clearly that he wasn't letting any more air in that week. Serge seized a wicker-covered bottle of the Chianti type and tapped him smartly on the crown. Dovebasket was not going to be treated like a breakfast egg by his hated rival. He dotted him back. This was fatal. One could see at once how wars break out. Poland and Rumania came to the Assistance of Serge, while Canada and Australia answered the call of the Mother Country. It looked like some strange Saturnalia, armed dips circling each other with wicker-covered bottles.

But as the fighting spread, Dovebasket got shifted from his perch and the life-giving H_2SO_4 began to pour once more into the cave. It was only just in time, I should say. The cellar now looked like a series of whimsical details from a Victorian canvas—I'm thinking of "Kiss Me Hardy" with Nelson down for the count in the Victory's cockpit. Some were kneeling in pleading postures. Some were crawling about in that painstaking way that beetles do when they are drunk on sugar-water. Others had simply keeled over among the flowers. The musicians drooped over their timbrels without enough oxygen between them for a trumpet-call or a groggy drum-tap. Then all of us, suddenly realizing, set up a shout and hurled ourselves towards the life-distributing oxygen pump.

With your permission I will draw a veil over the disgraceful scenes that ensued among the combatants. Dovebasket was knocked out. The Canadian Air Attaché had a collar-bone bruised. The egregious Serge escaped unscathed. A number of bottles were broken. Such language. Life has its ugly side, I suppose. But the main thing was that the Corps lived again, breathed again, could hold up its aching head once more. But one is hardly trained to live dangerously. Nevertheless, I noticed that not one dip failed to make a note of the wine of his choice. It would have been too much to miss that free crate. Some, in default of pencil and paper, had managed to scribble on their dickeys with lipstick. Polk-Mowbray, though beaten to his knees, nevertheless had the presence of mind to write Stella Polaris 1942 on his. Bloody, but relatively unbowed, you see.

And, as a matter of fact, after prayers the next day it was he who summed it all up rather neatly by saying: "And remember that in Peace, in War, in Love and in Diplomacy one thing is needful. I do not, I think, need to tell you what that is."

He didn't. It would have been labouring the point. We knew only too well. The Stiff Upper Lip.

A two-to-one Martini

Something à la Carte?

The tragedy of Mungo Piers-Foley is one (said Antrobus) which should give every Thoughtful Person Pause. It did me. It still does. By the purest inadvertency he found himself cast into the Bottomless Pit. He was a bit absent-minded that day. Yet what happened to him could happen to any of us.

Mungo was posted to us from the Blues as Military Attaché, and he was a gallant and carefree young colonel, full of the spice of life. You felt that he had a rich inner nature if only he could be persuaded to open his mouth. He was one of those mournful cylindrical men with hair parted in the middle—men who say little but think a lot. Yet who knows what they think? I don't. But he was an officer and a gentleman of unblemished reputation and a sportsman to boot. Not only to boot, to saddle as well. He had what is known as a splendid seat. He rode to hounds. However pointless the point-to-point, Mungo would be there, clearing hurdle after hurdle on his thoroughbred mule. He played polo without ever once hitting his horse. Myself I don't know much about horses, and what little I know seems to me singularly charmless. The last time I went hacking with Polk-Mowbray I got left in a tree for roughly the same reasons as Absalom. But that is neither here nor there. . . .

Mungo had won a huge collection of cups and saucers which he wore on his mantelpiece. He shot. He dynamited fish. An all-round sportsman if ever there was one. We were proud of him in the Mission. All this, of course, only made his tragedy harder cheese than ever. It happened while he was in Paris for a week to help reorganize the NATO cavalry to face the threat of a rocket age. On the morning of his return he lurched into my office looking like a lot of overlooked washing-up. "Antrobus," he said, "Hear my story. I am finished, old thing, absolutely finished. I've just put in my resignation and left Polk-Mowbray in tears." He sat down and fumbled for one of my cigars.

"It happened while I was in Paris," he said. "Quite inadvertent, the whole dashed thing. It could have happened to anyone. I popped into the Octagon for a bite. It wasn't until the *addition* came that I realized. Old man, *I had eaten a piece of horse!*"

I sprang up, startled. "You *what*?" I cried incredulously, realizing that I was in the presence of tragedy.

"Horse," he repeated wearily, passing his hand over his forehead. "As I live, Antrobus, a slice carved from a gee-gee. It all seems like a horrible dream. Yet I must say it cut quite sweetly and the sauce was so dashed good that I didn't realize it. It was only when the bill came that the whole of my past life flashed before my eyes. Dear God— a horse! And I a Colonel in the Blues! I was so surprised you could have poured me out with a spoon."

SOMETHING *À LA CARTE*?

I groaned in sympathy. He gave a harsh cracked laugh and went on. "To think of it, I who have lived for, and practically on, horses. The irony of it all. To find myself sitting there, involuntarily wrapped round a succulent slice of fetlock, feeling the world's biggest bounder. And with a touch of mustard, too." He shuddered at the memory.

"But surely," I said, looking as always for the Silver Lining, "you are hardly to be blamed, Mungo. Surely you could have absorbed just one slice and then Hushed Everything Up? No-one could find it in his heart to blame you."

He shook his head sadly. "I thought of that," he said, "but my conscience wouldn't give me any rest, Antrobus. After all, here I am, a founder-member of the Society For The Prevention Of Everything To Nags. Old Boy, I was largely instrumental in getting all those country houses set aside for aged horses, for getting them into the Health Service, for getting them painted by Munnings before they Passed On. Why, we were hoping to get one into Parliament this year. . . . How could I strike my colours, go back on my basic principles? I admit I thought of it. After all, I have eaten many strange things in unguarded moments. I once ate some smoked grandmother in the Outer Celebes, but that was to save the regimental goat. And once at Government House in Gibraltar I *think* I ate a portion of infant monkey. But it was never proved. The A.D.C. refused to confess. But all this is a far cry from horses, old chap. A different world. No, I confess that I sobbed aloud as I paid that bill."

For a moment he was silent, and then went on. "After that, Antrobus, there came an endless chain of sleepless nights. I brooded, old man. No peace. At times I thought I might go and throw myself on the mercy of Elizabeth

David, confessing everything to her frankly, hiding nothing, asking for absolution. But when I mugged up her books I found no references to anything more questionable than eels or bloater paste—revolting enough, but mundane compared to what I was up against. No, there was no way out. I realized that I should have to Face the Music. So I did. I confess it hurt. I resigned from Whites and Boodlès. I had myself crossed off every Stud Book in the Shires. The Athenaeum will see me no more. I even closed my account with the Army, Navy and Air-Force Stores. I transferred my overdraft. I confessed all to the Pytchley and did a public penance at Hurlingham. Then I broke my saddle over my knee . . . and all was over. I am a broken man, Antrobus. I simply came back to collect my gongs and brasses. I only popped in to say good-bye. I somehow felt you would understand."

I was deeply moved. But what could I say to comfort and console poor Mungo? Little enough in all conscience. He still had a fortnight to carry his bat until a replacement arrived and all this time he spent in strict purdah, refusing all invitations. There was only one little incident which, in the light of subsequent events, seems to me significant. It proved how deeply he had been marked by this Major Experience. His inhibitions had begun to slough off. De Mandeville reported that Mungo had been seen in a local hotel dining on *octopus*. I could hardly believe it. *Octopus!* The stuff that comes like ectoplasm! But this was the only straw in the wind. After that, silence closed in. Then Mungo left us and passed out of memory. As the years went by I often thought of him with a twinge of compassion. Doubtless he was in some far-enough-flung colony to dine openly on yams and white mice. I saluted his gallantry in my heart.

SOMETHING *À LA CARTE*?

But now here is the grisly sequel to my tale. Spalding used to go to Kenya every year to see his family and shoot a bit. One year he went up-country on *safari*. In the heart of the jungle, in a clearing, before a modest hut of wattle, he came upon a dinner-jacketed figure having a pre-prandial. "Mungo!" he cried. Yes, it was Mungo. He had hidden his shame in that remote corner. They embraced warmly and Spalding was glad to see that his character still had a few fibres intact—for he was correctly dressed for dinner. They sat down on camp-stools and discussed a two-to-one Martini which Mungo mixed with all his old *flair*. Though he had aged he still looked fairly steady on his pins, and he still made the sort of Martini which fairly whistles through the rigging. Heartening signs, these.

It was only when the brain-fever birds began to call and the little radio in the corner struck eight o'clock that Spalding Suddenly Understood that it wasn't, it couldn't be, the old Mungo. . . . For his host said, quite distinctly: "Why not stay and have pot-luck with me tonight? We have elephant for dins." *Elephant!*

Spalding paled—he had been very strictly brought up. Was it possible that Mungo was sitting out here in the wilds gorging himself on elephant? (And if so, how was it done? It must take ages to marinate?) He gulped loudly. "Did I understand you to say elephant, Mungo?" he said.

"Yes," said Mungo, with a kind of loose grin. "You see, old boy, there is no such thing as a *cuisine* in Africa. Once one leaves the Old Country one achieves a kind of Universality, a Oneness with Nature. HERE EVERY-THING IS EDIBLE." He spread his arms to the night, knocking over his glass. "If you don't like elephant," he went on, "I can organize squirrel or chipmunk or boa-constrictor. It's all one. I just send out a little man with a blow-pipe and it's all yours."

Spalding shuddered and muttered a prayer under his breath. "Yes," went on Mungo, "I gave away my Boulestin and both my Elizabeth David's. They are no use here except for missionaries who have Outworn Concepts. Personally I use Buffon's Natural History to give me ideas for my meals. Why, just to leaf through Section One (Primates) stimulates the appropriate juice, gives one an appetite. I say, you've turned awfully pale. You aren't ill, are you?"

"No, no," said Spalding, "it is simply the kerosene light shining on my rather high and pale forehead."

Mungo settled himself on his camp-stool and said: "Yes, old boy. If once the readers of *The Times* found out just how Edible everything is, it would be all up with the Wine and Food Society." Then in a slow, dreamy voice, full of naked *luxe* and *volupté*, he began to recite softly: "Leeches *à la rémoulade*. . . . Giraffe *Truffée aux Oignons*. . . . Boa-constrictor *Chasseur*. . . . *Ragoût de Flamingo* with *Water-Rat Flambé*. . . ." He was sunk in a deep trance.

Spalding could bear it no longer. He tip-toed out of the clearing and ran like a madman in the direction of Nairobi. . . .

Now I didn't tell you this story (said Antrobus) simply to upset you. No. Moreover, I hope you won't repeat it. I should hate it to get back to the Household Cavalry. It simply illustrates the sort of thing one is up against in the Service. The next Christmas, when my Aunt Hetty asked me to choose two quotations for a sampler she was making me, it was really with Mungo in mind that I made my choice. One text reads: "By their Menus shall ye know them." And the other: "Nothing Exceeds like Excess". . . .

I trust you take my point?

Polk-Mowbray got a terrific electric shock

The Unspeakable Attaché

It was (said Antrobus) a bit before your time—mercifully for you. The creature was posted just before you arrived. Now of this fellow, Trevor Dovebasket (he was then assistant Military Attaché), I have only this to say: it was clear that the youth was in league with the Devil. Some fearful Faustian compact had taken place. You could tell from his appearance—eyebrows meeting in the middle. It was clear from the way that he bit his nails that he read *Popular Mechanics* in secret. More, his office was always full of meccano and string. He was always tampering with electrical circuits, fuses, and using that beastly sticky stuff and so on. A really vicious streak. One day Polk-Mowbray got a terrific electric shock off his telephone. Then some Juliets exploded under the noses of the Rotary Club causing grave loss of morale. It was never proved, of course, but I knew. . . . Something told me it was Dovebasket.

He was in league with the Devil on one side and De Mandeville on the other. Together they organized a form of beetle-racing in the Chancery. Beetles with electro-magnets tied to their tails, if you please. Imagine my concern. The beetles were named after us. They made a book and encouraged betting wholesale. Dolly Pusey, the new cipherine, gambled away a year's unearned increments and most of the fruits of the F.O. Pension Scheme in a matter of minutes. When I found out I had no option but to return her to London. But that was not all. . . .

They invented an electric train for serving food and sold the idea to Drage as a labour-saving device. The train ran on to the dining-table and stopped before the diners with a plate on each carriage. On the face of it it seemed ingenious. It was worked by buttons from Polk-Mowbray's place. Mind you, I had my doubts. But as there was an Electrical Trades Union Conference and we had some of its members to lunch Polk-Mowbray (who had a childish streak) thought he would impress them with his little toy. You have guessed? It was not until the *Bombe Surprise* was loaded that the machinery went wrong. There was a frightful accident, the train was de-railed into our laps, and the *Bombe* (a marvellous creation on which Drage had spent all night) lived up to its name . . . De Mandeville got Number One Field Punishment. He had to feed the goldfish in the Residence for a month.

Well, this is only to show you what I was up against with this fellow Dovebasket. At this time the Corps was going through one of its Little Phases. Dips are a somewhat emulous tribe as you know, always trying to vie with one another. That winter it was dogs. The Hungarians led off. Their Labour Attaché suddenly appeared with some colossal greyhounds from the Steppes. He allowed himself to be towed about in public by them wearing a somewhat fanciful air. At once everyone got

emulous. In a matter of weeks the dog market was boom-
ing. Everyone had dogs of various sizes and shapes: huge
ones, little ones, squashed-looking ones and ones that
looked like cold rissoles. The French went in for topiary
jobs, the Italians for the concertina shape, the British for
those great torpid brutes which carry Hennessy's Brandy
round in artful little barrels. I forget their names. They
rescue people from snowdrifts by licking their faces and
dealing out a much-needed tot at the right time. Horrible. The Albanians produced some green-fanged sheep-
dogs so fierce that they had to be kept tied to trees in the
grounds and fed by a system of underarm bowling until
a shepherd was found who understood their natures. He
took them for walks on a length of steel hawser.

Well, this was all very well, had not Polk-Mowbray
been fired by the idea of a Diplomatic Dog-Show. He was
always easily led and this fellow Dovebasket fired him
with thoughts of winning a first prize in the barrel-push-
ing class. I viewed the whole thing with concern, but I
could not guess from which quarter the blow might fall.
Anyway, they worked out a splendid dog-show at which
every Mission would win the first prize of its class and
all our honours be simultaneously saved. Rosettes, buttons, marking-cards—everything was thought out. A
firm of dog-biscuit manufacturers was persuaded to put
up some rather depressing prizes in the form of dog-
statuettes in pressed steel which De Mandeville painted
with gold leaf to make look more expensive. The Town
Hall was engaged for the *venue* and the press was fed with
a great deal of advance information in the form of news-
flashes which it did not use. Speeches were carefully
worked up containing the requisite number of Tactful
Phrases about Everything. The ladies of the Corps de-

cided to make it a contest of dresses as well as dogs. Many were the clever little creations run up overnight, many the models flown from Paris. The air was full of excitement. It was the first Spring engagement. Sewing machines hummed night and day. The Minister For Interior was invited to give away the prizes—there was one for each Chief Of Mission. Polk-Mowbray went through agonies of excitement practising his Few Words Of Thanks in the Residence pier-glass. Altogether it looked like a pleasurable and harmonious afternoon. But . . . there was a look in Dovebasket's eye I misliked. Could it be, I wondered, that the fellow was Up To Something? One never knew. I confess that there was a still small voice within me which whispered "Something is bound to give" as I studied the (I must say) very creditable lay-out of the Town Hall, gay with the flags of every nation and made brilliant by the courtly presence of Our Ladies in their prettiest frocks. The day was fine and sunny. The dogs were extremely even tempered, wagging their grotesque stumps and coloured ribbons as the solemn group of judges circulated marking down points on their embossed cards. Cocktails were coming up thick and fast.

It was at this point that I distinctly heard De Mandeville say in the hoarse undertone. "Let her go now, Dovie." Together the two retreated to a high stand above the *mêlée* while a look of intense interest came over their faces. Dovebasket appeared to have a cold and put a handkerchief to his face. He appeared to blow his nose. Suddenly a quiver of anguish appeared to run through the canine population like a wind in corn. The Albanian sheep-dogs gave one long quivering howl like an Alban Berg violin solo and then . . . all hell broke loose. These peaceable amiable dogs suddenly turned upon their masters and the judges, seething with an inexplicable rage. They turned upon one another. Cries and tumult arose. Stands were overturned. The sheep dogs went into action against the Labradors, the Airedales against the Fox terriers. Owners were dragged hither and thither by their leashes which got inextricably mixed up with chairs and legs and dips. Bites of all sizes and depths were registered. Blood began to flow, tempers to rise. The Russians began to shake their fists. The Minister was bitten in his . . . seat of office. Polk-Mowbray lost a spat to a shaggy mixed-up Borzoi. Lap-dogs squealed like piccolos, the bigger brutes bayed, the diplomats moaned, positively moaned.

In a single bound I was at Dovebasket's side. I whipped the handkerchief from his face. "Unmasked," I hissed. It was just as I thought. He was blowing hard upon one of those whistles which, while inaudible to the human ear, produced a high-pitched buzz calculated to unnerve dogs. "It was simply an experiment," he said with a sickly smile, "De Mandeville betted me an even tenner that my whistle wouldn't work."

"Experiment!" I cried. "Look around you, you wretched youth." The scene was a terrible one to witness. I have not seen anything to equal it—except perhaps once when someone released a grass-snake at a Pen Club Conference in Venice. I turned upon Dovebasket. "Give me that foul instrument," I cried in a voice of thunder. "I confiscate it. And as soon as it is safe to get down I shall conduct you to your Chief of Mission."

But he only smirked. He was incorrigible, the little blackhead. When later that day I told Polk-Mowbray about the whistle he was beside himself with rage. "Dove-

basket must go," he said in ringing tones. And duly—
these things take an age to arrange—Dovebasket went.
He was promoted to the rank of Senior Military Attaché
in Delhi. Upwards, old boy. It's always upwards in the
service. That is perhaps the tragedy of it all.

A titanic battle now began

The Game's the Thing

As for Sport (said Antrobus), the very word makes me uneasy. I've never believed in its healing power. Once I was forced to referee a match between H.M.S. Thread-bare and the French Fleet which resulted in my nearly being dismembered. Luckily the Gents in the pavilion had a bolt and padlock on it or I wouldn't be here today. No. I regard Sport with Grave Reserve.

Polk-Mowbray was not of my opinion; he believed in the stuff. Thereby hangs my tale. It was during one of those long unaccountable huffs between ourselves and the Italians. You know the obscure vendettas which break out between Missions? Often they linger on long after the people who threw the first knife have been posted away. I have no idea how this huff arose. I simply inherited it from bygone dips whose bones were now dust. It was in full swing when I arrived—everyone applying freezing-mixture to the Italians and getting the Retort Direct in exchange. When you saw an Italian at a party you gave a slow smile amputated by scorn. Yes, we made it clear that we were pretty miffed about something. They also acted in a markedly miffed manner. Yet I doubt if anyone on either side could have explained why we were all so dashed miffed. So while bows were still exchanged for protocol reasons they were only, so to speak, from above the waist. A mere contortion of the dickey, if you take me, as a tribute to manners. A slight Inclination accompanied by a *moue*. Savage work, old lad, savage work!

One day, however, the wind changed. Polk-Mowbray called a senior conference. "We must end this huff," he said regretfully. "Though it goes against the grain. London says that these dastards are going to vote against us at UNO. We must put aside our private pleasures and do everything to soothe and mollify the dogs. Our duty calls on us to surrender Our All." Several ideas for promoting the peace were put up, and at last—O fatal Dovebasket! —there came one which fired Polk-Mowbray's imagination." That's it!" he cried. "Brilliant! Magistral! Prescient! Dovebasket, I salute you! You will go far."

The idea was this: to challenge the Italian Mission to a football match and lose it gracefully, thus making them feel happy and well-disposed. Now everyone knew that the Italian Chancery was staffed by three guards who had been professionals once—footballers of international pointlessness. The team was a formidable one. To this we would oppose a scratch team of dead-beat dips who would be run off their feet in quarter of an hour, thus losing by two hundred goals to nothing. Like all Dovebasket's schemes it seemed sound on the face of it, almost ingenious. I had an obscure premonition of doom but I brushed it aside. What could go wrong with such an idea ? I did not of course know (none of us did) that two of our own Chancery Guards, Morgan and Bolster, were also internationals and had played for Wales. Furthermore I did not know that Dovebasket was short of money. True he was always hanging about the Chancery sucking the silver head of a swagger-stick and saying: "I'm fearfully pushed for lolly these days." I paid no attention, being somewhat pushed myself. Afterwards it all became clear. Dovebasket and De Mandeville were in league. No sooner was the match declared on than they began taking bets *against* instead of *for* the Italians.

Innocently we pushed on with our preparations for this senseless frolic unaware of the trap they were setting for us. Polk-Mowbray spent quite a lot of money from the Secret Service Vote to buy us blue shorts with a polka-dot design and singlets of red-white-and-blue. I don't suppose we made much of a showing as we bowled on to the field to the polite hand-claps of the Ladies of the Corps. Most of us had that dreadful rinsed-out look which comes from Conferences. We had all constructed heavy shin-pads from the Master-Files. I had nearly a week's economic despatches down each stocking. Of course with all this defensive equipment we moved like pregnant water-buffaloes. Without grace, without poetry. But we tried to look as if we meant business.

I must say the three Italian forwards filled me with the liveliest anxiety. They were very large indeed and I noticed that they had long-handled knives in their stockings. I was rather glad that we were all set to lose. The two Ambassadors elected to goal-keep because Heads of Mission don't like to be seen hurrying. All were at last assembled. The pitch was ankle deep in mud and within a moment the ball resembled a half-mixed cake so that even Arturo, Benjamino and Luigi had some difficulty in pushing it about. It was even harder for us. After a few minutes of desultory running about we were all pretty winded and dispersed while the Italians executed some dashing figures of eight all round us, steadily moving down upon the anxious Polk-Mowbray—remorseless as an enema, old man.

Our defence was of the open-work variety and within a very few minutes they had scored a goal. Then another. Then another. Everyone beamed and resisted an impulse to cheer. We embraced them. They embraced us. Polk-Mowbray insisted on planting a fraternal kiss upon the Italian Ambassador's cheek. He, poor man, was deeply moved and clearly no longer miffed in the least. You can say what you like but we British know how to lose gamely. Prefer it, in fact. We had all taken on that frightfully decent look as we puffed about, showing ourselves plucky but inept—in fact in character. Our ladies cheered shrilly and waved their umbrellas.

By half-time we were seven goals down. Singularly few mishaps had occurred. True the Naval Attaché on the wing (who believed in reincarnation) was badly hacked by a free-thinking third secretary, but nobody gave a fig about that. We were losing, that was the main thing. It was not until half-time that Dovebasket's dastardly plan came into action. He and De Mandeville gracefully circulated the refreshments—rum cocktails and acid drops—before announcing their intention of retiring from the game "to give the replacements a chance". Both, it seemed, had slipped a disc. Polk-Mowbray was sympathetic, suspected nothing. "What bad luck," he cried. And as the whistle went I saw the military attaché's jeep approaching among the trees with the replacements in it. Two huge figures—Morgan and Bolster—sat in the back, armed *cap à pie* for the fray. "Well, well, Chancery Guards," cried Polk-Mowbray democratically. "What an awfully good show! That will freshen us up." Little did he know. . . .

They were huge, old man. I'd never seen them undressed before, so to speak. Such thews. Knotted and gnarled. Real Henry Moore jobs both. And covered in tattooing as well—ships and crowns and girl-friends' phone-numbers. Worst of all they both wore an air of surly magnificence that can only come from long leisurely potions of Navy Issue rum. They gave off waves of jaunty and illicit self-confidence. My heart began to sink as I watched these case-hardened male-nurses come trotting across the bog to take their place in our forward line. My blood froze as I heard Morgan whisper hoarsely: "Now remember we've got to do them proper or Dovie won't give us our cut, see?" So that was it! A cry broke from my lips. It was drowned by the whistle. We were off like men struggling for life in an ocean of glue.

What a titanic battle now began between the opposing forwards! The collisions in mid-air, the feints, the sorties, the trapeze-acts! Our innocent little game of push-ball suddenly took on a starker aspect; it was becoming more like a medieval butchery in a tilt-yard. The compatriots of Toscanini sent up musical cries of amazement at this sudden passionate flowering of a skill they did not guess we owned. By a brilliant system of double-entry Morgan and Bolster shot four goals in just over five minutes. Polk-Mowbray began to look faintly alarmed. The Italians, recovering from their surprise, buckled down to the job. The barges, the elbowing, the rabbit-punches on the referee's blind side began to increase. It was clear that we were losing our amateur status at last. Morgan and

41

Bolster were used to this. For them it was just like winding in a capstan. Counter-barges and counter-shoves followed with the occasional dull thwack of a rabbit-punch. Cries of, "Foul" and, "You keek me, yes?" Two more goals to our credit. "By thunder!" cried Polk-Mowbray passionately. "What is going on?" Well might he ask. Bolster and Morgan were now playing with the concentrated fury of religious fanatics who had glimpsed the Promised Land. I don't know how much money was at stake. The Italians too had begun to get pretty rough. The pace had also increased. Clash followed upon clash. "Great Heavens!" cried Polk-Mowbray feebly. "Have they not been briefed, the Guards?" Yes, they had; but alas, not in the intended sense.

There was ten minutes to go when Bolster equalized. A groan went up from Italians and British alike. The Italian Ambassador burst into tears. Arturo began to finger the knife in his stocking and mutter. I felt quite faint just looking at him. The whistle again. By now everyone seemed to have become infected by pure rage. I received a kick from De Ponzo (ordinarily the mildest of men, a father, a bird-watcher)—a kick which left traces. I'll show you some time. In fact from a diplomatic football match the thing was steadily becoming a spectacle of unbridled bestiality. Such pushing, such cuffing, such heaving and bumping I have never witnessed before or since. And the language—a Saturnalia of Swearing, old man. If I hadn't been so scared I would have blushed to the roots of my C.M.G. Then at last it came—the dire *coup de grâce*.

Bolster opened fire with a boom like a sixteen-inch gun right from the popping-crease as it were. There was cold and dire malevolence about the shot. The sodden leather fairly winged through the sky towards the uncorseted form of the Italian Chief Of Mission. Mind you, for an ethereal sort of man he was quite spirited and did not flinch. There was a hollow concussion followed by a yell as our distinguished colleague received the charge full in the midriff. I felt things going black all round me. What a shot! Yes, and what a casualty—for the poor Ambassador, propelled backwards through his own goal by the sheer force of this flying pudding, was soon lying senseless in the ditch. It seemed to me that all they could do now was to draw a mackintosh reverently over the body before resuming play—as they do at Twickenham. *We were now leading by one goal.* Imagine our despair! Polk-Mowbray was dancing with rage and consternation in our goalmouth. The ladies were screaming shrilly. Drage was holding a mirror to the Italian Ambassador's lips and shaking his head sadly. On all sides rose cries for help. Messengers began running in all directions for ambulances.

And it was now that the tactless Bolster cried merrily: "Another eight minutes to go." And this tore it, to use a vulgar phrase, tore it good and proper right down the centre. The Italian forwards closed in on him with the manifest intention of wiping the smile from his lips. Morgan intervened. Blows began to be exchanged. The Naval Attaché was struck down. Other peacemakers tried unwisely to intervene. The referee was gouged and swallowed the pea in his whistle. A scuffle now started destined to end in a riot. Knives were drawn. There were slashes and screams. The ladies shrieked in unison. It was nearly ten minutes before the Vulgarian Flying-Squad arrived and surged on to the pitch armed with tommy-guns. We were all under arrest. We were ignominiously

THE GAME'S THE THING

handcuffed together for nearly an hour before the *doyen* could persuade them that we were privileged dips and not subject to the civil penalties of riot. Those not on the list—our forwards and theirs—were carried away in a plain van. The whole thing ended in a scandal.

And our neat little plan? What is there to add? The vote went against us at UNO, and the Italians stayed miffed. To add insult to injury Dovebasket's Christmas Card that year showed a Father Xmas in football-boots. Yes, of course they stayed miffed. I bet you the miff remains unrequited to this day.

No, you'll never catch me joking about sport.

"Answer me at once, or in Heaven's name I'll——"

If Garlic be the Food of Love...

Every Wednesday now, in the winter, I lunch with Antrobus at his club, picking him up at the Foreign Office just before noon. I think he enjoys these meetings as much as I do for they enable him to reminisce about old times in the Foreign Service. For my part I am always glad to add an anecdote or two to my private *Antrobus File*—the groundwork upon which I one day hope to raise the monument of my own Diplomatic Memories. . . .

Yesterday his memory carried him back to Vulgaria again where he had served under Polk-Mowbray—and over De Mandeville—as Head of Chancery. "Bitter days," he mused. "And perhaps one shouldn't talk about them. De Mandeville was in a queer state all that spring; perhaps it had something to do with the phases of the moon? I don't know. He was in a "Hamlet, Revenge!" sort of mood. The trouble seemed to centre about the Embassy table—as Third Sec. he had a watching brief on the food. It started I remembered with a series of Constance Spry table-decorations which made that otherwise fairly festive board look like an illustration from the Jungle Books.

One could hardly carry a fork to one's mouth without biting off a piece of fern by mistake. Slices of decorative pumpkin and marrow gave a Harvest Festival note to things. One peered at one's guests through a forest of potted plants. Finally Polk-Mowbray put his foot down. De Mandeville became huffed. The next thing was he ordered Drage to serve everything from the right—in deference to a left-handed Trade Mission chief who was staying with us. It may have been tactful but it led to endless complications with us right-handed trenchermen who found everything upside down, and had to scuffle to rearrange our table-patterns as we sat down. And then what with Drage coming in so fast from the wrong side one was practically always out, hit-wicket on the *soufflé*. I tried to reason with De Mandeville but he only pouted and bridled. It was clear that he was in an ugly mood, old boy. I feared the worst. I have a sort of intuition about these things.

"The next thing in this chain of progressive sabotage was curry. De Mandeville had a series of Madras curries served. They were of such a blistering intensity that the entire Dutch Embassy had the inside of its collective mouth burned away—peeled off like bark from a tree, old boy. The Minister called on Polk-Mowbray in *tenue* and wanted to know if a state of war existed between England and Holland. His wife had to be treated for soft palate. A junior attaché went about saying that the Embassy food was full of quicklime and hinting darkly about damages. Naturally there were high words and massive contempts flying about which made Polk-Mowbray somewhat nervy. De Mandeville was sharply taken to task, but without avail. He next served an onion soup and black bread without soup-spoons. You know how long a rich onion

48

soup takes to cool. Our little lunch-party dragged on almost to dusk, and several guests were lightly scalded because they neglected to take thermometer readings before gulping. The whole thing was gradually working up towards a climax. I saw it all coming and mentally, so to speak, closed my eyes and breathed a prayer to the Goddess of Diplomacy. I could not, however, guess from which quarter this warped and twisted Third Sec. might deliver the knock-out blow.

"Then . . . all this is in the strictest confidence, old man. . . . Then it came. Polk-Mowbray used to leave his office door wide open so I could see and hear all that went on therein. One morning I heard a familiar sort of row going on and I knew that the blow had fallen at last. Polk-Mowbray was hysterical. 'I adjure you by the bones of Cromer', he was yelling, 'to answer me without prevarication. *Have you been putting garlic in the food without telling anyone?* Did you, wittingly or unwittingly plug that *cassoulet*, impregnate that lustreless salad, order the peas to be lightly simmered in the stuff before serving? Answer me at once, or in Heaven's Name I'll——'

"De Mandeville made a gobbling self-deprecating sort of sound and spread his manicured hands as he muttered something about garlic being eaten in all the best London houses. It toned up the nervous system. Some said it was the only specific for scabies. One would have to be very retrograde to imagine. . . . And so on in this style. Veins were throbbing all over poor Polk-Mowbray by this time. 'Do not try to justify yourself,' he thundered. 'Answer me with a simple yea or nea. And take that beastly sensual smile off your face. If you choose to dine on heads of raw garlic with your scabrous chauffeur it is your business. But the Embassy table is sacred, do you hear? *Sacred.* If you do not answer truthfully I shall make you the subject of a General Paper to the Foreign Secretary.' There was a short silence during which they glared at each other. Then De Mandeville threw back his chin and uttered the word 'yes' rather defiantly; he was wearing an obstinate Canine Defence League expression on his face. Polk-Mowbray levitated briefly and banged his desk with a triumphant. 'Aha! So you *did.*' It was clear that De Mandeville was in for one of those Searching Reproofs. His Chief now began to walk up and down his own carpet as he always did when he was moved. He Pointed The Finger Of Scorn at De Mandeville in no uncertain fashion. 'Wretch!' he cried in a shaking voice. 'Could you not see the harm that might come from such reckless and criminal cookery? Moreover you choose the *one* lunch party of the year which is of policy importance in order to do me the greatest damage. Think of the Naval Attaché! What has he ever done to merit that unspeakable lunch—at which he ate far too heartily? And my niece Angela—what of her? And the Head of the Foreign Ministry—what of him?'

"De Mandeville tried to make a few unavailing protests. 'Enough!' cried Polk-Mowbray hoarsely. 'Surely you know that to feed a Naval Attaché garlic is like stoking a coke furnace with dead rats? Did you see his face as he lurched out into the afternoon? You did not know, I suppose, that he was due to lecture to the Sea Wolves on Temperance and Self-Denial at sea? He created a very poor impression in a very short time. The wretch now fears court-martial. He says that now whenever his pinnace is sighted they raise a Yellow Fever flag and forbid him access to the ship. I do not doubt that the dirk-point will be facing him when he walks into the ward-room. All this is on your head and more. Don't interrupt me. That is not all. Do you realize that when I helped the Minister into his car he was making a noise like a bunsen burner? *You* would not care that he had to address the High Praesidium that afternoon on Foreign Affairs—moreover in a language so full of aspirates as to make the gravest demands on his audience! No, *you* would not care, with your pumpkins and pottery and left-handed table arrangements! On you go in your headlong career, weaving these devilish plots around my table. And apart from all this what about *me*. *You* cannot be expected to know that I was booked to read the Lesson at a Memorial Service in the British Baptist Chapel which is notoriously cramped and ill-ventilated. How did you think I felt when I saw the first two rows of the congregation swaying like ripened wheat in an east wind? How do you think I felt when it came to my turn to embrace the hapless widow? She was breathing as if she had slipped her fan-belt. Answer me! You see, you haven't a word to say. You are mumchance as you jolly well ought to be. Fie on you, Aubrey de Mandeville! *You* did not stop to think what effect Angela might have on Cosgrave after such a lunch. The engagement was pretty tremulous as it was— but you snookered the wretched girl well and truly. And what of the typists' pool? Girls keeling over one after another as they tried to take dictation from us. What of them?' For a moment words failed him. His face worked. Then he said in a low murderous tone, from between clenched teeth. 'I tell you that from now on there is to be no more garlic. Sage, yes. Thyme, yes. Rosemary, marjoram, dill, cummin, yes. Emphatically yes. But *garlic*, no!' And so the edict went forth and the sale of peppermints in the Naafi dropped off again."

IF GARLIC BE THE FOOD OF LOVE . . .

Antrobus sighed sadly over these memories as he replenished our glasses. Then he said musingly: "I should say really that Garlic was the biggest Single Cross a Diplomat had to bear in the rough old times. It *had* to be banned, old man. Yet in a sense we were all Living A Lie, like the Americans under Prohibition; for we all secretly yearned after the stuff. (I say this in the strictest confidence. I would not wish to be quoted.) Yet it is strange that this noxious bulb should have such an allure for men. As for diplomats, it played havoc with Confidential Exchanges; and as for dancing with your Ambassadress . . . well. It was the quickest way to get posted. That is why I was so relieved when the Age Of Science dawned. I used to be *against* Science once, and for the Humanities—I freely admit it. But when at last chlorophyl came in I was instantly won over. What a boon and a blessing to dips! What an over-riding sense of relief! Many a breach was healed that day between man and man. Even Polk-Mowbray in the end allowed the salad-bowl to be lightly rubbed with a couple of heads before serving. And I don't know whether you noticed the rather respectable little *ragoût* we have just been eating? Not bad for the Club, is it? But fear nothing! In my pocket lies a phial full of those little grey tablets which make human intercourse a rational, easy, unbuttoned sort of thing again. No more shrinking from pursed lips in The Office. We can hold our heads high once more! Let's drink a final little toast to the Goddess of the F.O. shall we? I give you Chlorophyll!"

The F.O.'s senior courier running howling across the town

6

Where the Bee Sucks...

One is at a loss (said Antrobus) when one looks back on those rough old times to account for the thin but rich vein of fatuity which ran through the character of Polk-Mowbray. Though in many ways an admirable Chief of Mission, a talented and self-disciplined man, nevertheless, he was in others simply a babe in arms, old boy, a babe in arms.

The main thing I think was that he was subject to Sudden Urges. He was over-imaginative, he was highly-strung. One week for example it would be Sailors' Knots. It was all right so long as he only sat at his desk playing with string but this was not all. He grew reckless, ambitious, carried away by all this new knowledge. He took to demonstrating his powers at children's parties, charity bazaars, cocktails—everywhere. And the awful thing was that his tricks never worked. He trussed the German Ambassador's eldest son up so tightly that the child nearly suffocated; we just released him in time with the help of the garden shears. Drage had to pour a pail of sweet iced Cup all over the little swollen Teuton face to revive the brat. Then Polk-Mowbray tied himself to the Embassy door-knob and could not disengage. Quite a crowd gathered. It was humiliating. Once more we had to resort to the shears. I took to keeping a pair of them handy in my office. As Head of Chancery you can imagine how my responsibilities weighed upon me. . . .

"Antrobus," he used to say to me as he sat abstractedly making love-knots in a length of high quality manila. "Antrobus I am in the wrong profession. Only just realized it. I should have been sent to sea as a youth. Round the Cape in a sou'wester, what? That should have been my life, Antrobus." Who was I, as his junior, to contradict?

Two days later I came in to find his typist spliced to the Chancery radiator by one swollen wrist. She was in tears. Polk-Mowbray could not release her and nor could I. "Tut tut," he kept saying. "And such a simple little running bowline too. It is most vexing. I was just trying to show Angela a wrinkle or two." In the end, Morgan the Chancery guard was forced to pull the radiator out of the wall to free her. Water poured out into De Mandeville's office and ruined a Persian carpet he prized. Obviously things had gone far enough. We had a secret meeting and delegated to Butch Benbow, the Naval Attaché, the task of crushing this little hobby before the whole Corps was infected by it. We knew that in his present mood Polk-Mowbray reverenced all seafaring men—even if they were martyrs to sea-sickness as Butch Benbow was. . . . I must say, though, he was clever, was Butch. But then you can always count on the Navy. He asked Polk-Mowbray outright whether he wasn't *afraid* to go on playing with string at such a rate—and on such a scale?

WHERE THE BEE SUCKS . . .

"Afraid?" said the Chief Of Mission mildly. "Why afraid?"

"The last Ambassador to suffer from stringomania", said Butch earnestly, "hung himself." He went *krik krik* with his mouth and drew a string round his neck with his finger. Then, to complete the pantomime he rolled his eyes up into his skull until only the whites showed and stuck out a large—and I must say somewhat discoloured and contused tongue. "He's quite right, sir," I said. Polk-Mowbray looked from one to the other, quite startled. "But sailors do it all the time," he said.

"Sailors can untie themselves when they wish," said Butch somewhat stiffly. "Besides they don't walk in their sleep like you do, sir. The Ambassador I spoke of was also a sleep-walker." This really made Polk-Mowbray jump. It was one of those lucky hits. Actually he had only once walked in his sleep—though the result was disastrous. I'll tell you about it sometime. It was after a prawn curry devised by De Mandeville. He sat staring at us for a long time with popping eye. Then he sighed regretfully and we knew that for him the days of sail were numbered.

"Thank you for your solicitude," he said.

Well, that was only an example: I really wanted to tell you about the infernal bees. One day I walked into his office and found him clad for the most part in a bee-keeper's veil and gauntlets and holding a sort of tuning-fork with which, as I understand it, you pick up the Queen. I was aghast, but he only waved airily and told me to sit down. "Antrobus," he said, "I have the answer to the monotony of this post. The murmur of innumerable bees, dear boy. A *pastoral* hobby, suitable for diplomats. Something that harms no-one, and which yields honey

for tea." All around him lay magazines and brochures
entitled *Profitable Bee Keeping, The Hornet and Bee Guide,
The Bee-Fancier*—and that sort of thing. It was clear that
he had been delving deeply into bee lore. "I have ordered
a hive from Guernsey," he said, "and asked the Bag
Room to send them on." "The Bag Room," I faltered.
"But surely livestock is on the proscribed list?" The
people who make up the Diplomatic Bag as you know
are pretty touchy and there are endless rules and regula-
tions about what you can and can't send by bag. Polk-
Mowbray shook his head. "I've looked up the regula-
tions," he said, "there is nothing about bees. The chief
prohibition is on liquids, but a hive of bees isn't liquid."
I doubted the soundness of his reasoning. Liquids were
proscribed because once in the old days a young attaché
had sent a bottle of inferior Chianti back to his mother
and it had exploded. Most of Lord Cromer's despatches
had to be hung out to dry before serving, and some of
them actually turned green. The bottle must have been
sinfully corked. But then Italian wine. . . . Anyway, I still
didn't like to think of the Bag Room trustingly accepting
a cardboard box with a few holes in the top. "What if they
make honey among the confidential despatches?" I said.
He laughed airily. "Pouf!" he said. "There will be no
difficulty about that. You will see."

I said no more. Seven days later a disgraceful scene
took place on the platform at Venice. The bees, mad-
dened by their solitude in the bag, broke out and stormed
into the first-class carriage where Fothergill the courier
was eating a ham sandwich. They stung him. He, poor
fellow, was attached by a padlock to the sack and could
not free himself in time. The next thing was the spectacle
of the F.O.'s senior courier running howling across the

town waving a bag out of which poured bees and confidential reports in ever increasing quantities. The other couriers, in a vain attempt to help followed him in a sort of demonic paper-chase which only ended at St. Marks, where Fothergill took sanctuary behind the altar. Here the darkness foxed the bees and they turned their attention to the priests. And our mail? Old man, it was all at the bottom of the Grand Canal. The consul general was forced to set out with a fleet of gondolas to rescue it before it fell into Unauthorized Hands. You can imagine what a scandal. Fothergill arrived beeless and bagless and under a threat of Excommunication. I thought this would cure Polk-Mowbray. Not a bit. The next lot were sent out by air in an airtight container and Drage was sent to meet them at the airport. A hive had been rigged up in the garage and Polk-Mowbray walked about the Residence in his veil waiting for his blasted bees with feverish professional impatience. At last the moment came. He knew just how to tip them out, and so on. But the bees took violent exception to the hive and within a matter of seconds were darkening the sky. They flew round and round in a desultory fashion at first and then with a roar flew into a drainpipe and emerged in the Chancery where they settled in the old tin stove by the bookcase. For a while everyone was on guard but the little creatures were quite well behaved. "Live and let live," cried Polk-Mowbray sucking his thumb. (He had been stung.) "If the brutes want to live here we shall respect their wishes." "I thought it a bit hard on the junior secretaries but what could I say?

But somewhat to my surprise the bees gave no trouble whatsoever; indeed as time went on their subdued murmuring helped rather than hindered the composition of despatches. Polk-Mowbray rather lost interest in them: from time to time he would put on his veil and peer up the stove-pipe, calling upon them to be good boys and come out for a fly round, but much to everyone's relief they ignored him. Gradually nobody thought of them at all. But alas! This was not to be the end of the story. When the bees finally did emerge they created unparalleled havoc. It was all due to a new secretary, Sidney Trampelvis, who had been insufficiently briefed, and who, on a whim, filled the stove with old betting slips he no longer needed and blithely set them alight. Now at this time there was one of those Ineffably Delicate Conferences taking place in the committee-room, presided over by no less a personage than Lord Valerian—you know, the Treasury chap. It was all about a trade pact—I must not reveal the details. Now this fellow Valerian—rather a bounder I thought—for some reason awed Polk-Mowbray. I don't know why. Perhaps he had highly placed relations in the F.O. Perhaps it was his enormous beard which hung down like a fire curtain and only parted occasionally when he moved to reveal a strip of O.E. tie. Typical of course. The rumour was that he used to wear his O.E. tie in bed, over his pyjama jacket. Well, we Wykehamists can only raise a lofty eyebrow over this sort of gossip—which by the way we never repeat. Well, there we all were in solemn conclave when there arose a confused shouting from the Chancery where Trampelvis was receiving the first thrust, so to speak. There followed a moment of silence during which Valerian cleared his throat and was about to launch himself again, and then there came a tremendous hum followed by the sound of running feet. I did not know Drage was capable of such a turn of speed. Into the room he bounded—perhaps with some vague idea of saving his Chief, perhaps of issuing a general gale warning. But it was too late. They were upon us in a compact and lethal cloud, flying very low and with stings at the ready. The confusion was indescribable. Have you ever seen *bees* on a fighter sweep, old boy? Ever felt them crawling up your trousers, down your collar, into your waistcoat? One would have to have nerves of steel not to shriek aloud. To judge by the noises we started making it would be clear that diplomatic nerves are made not so much of steel as of raffia. People began beating themselves like old carpets. Polk-Mowbray after one plaintive cry of, "My bees," seized a poker and started behaving like Don Quixote with a set of particularly irritating windmills. Drage lapsed into Welsh religious verse punctuated by snarls and a sort of involuntary pole-jumping. I hid myself in the curtains and extinguished the bees as hard as I could. But the awful thing was that the Queen (I imagine it was her) made a bee-line (to coin a metaphor) for the Drury Lane beard of Lord Valerian who as yet had not fully grasped the situation. He looked down with ever-growing horror to find them swarming blithely in it, with the obvious intention of setting up house there. He was too paralysed to move. (I think personally that he used to spray his beard with Eau de Portugal before committee meetings and this must have attracted the Queen.) Mind you this all happened in a flash. Polk-Mowbray, what with guilt and solicitude for Valerian, was almost beside himself; no sacrifice, he felt, was too great to save the day. In a flash of gallantry he seized the garden shears which had been lying on the mantelpiece (pitiful relic of the days when he played with string) and with a manful though ragged snip . . . divested the Chairman of both beard and O.E. tie at one and the same stroke . . . I cannot say it improved Valerian's temper any more than his appearance—Polk-Mowbray had sliced rather badly. But there it was. Walking wounded had to retire to the buttery for a Witch Hazel compress. The bees, having done their worst, flew out of the window and into the Ministry of Foreign Affairs across the road. I did not wait to see the sequel. I was so grateful for emerging from this business unscathed that I tip-toed back to my office and rang down to the buttery. I don't mind admitting that I ordered a Scotch and Soda, and a stiffer one than usual. I would even admit (under pressure, and *sotto voce*) that you might have seen a faint, fugitive smile graven upon my lips. I was not entirely displeased, old man, with Polk-Mowbray's method of dealing with an O.E. tie. In my view it was the only one. Was it, I wondered, too much to hope that it might become More General?

"Just look around you"

7

Cry Wolf

"The case of Wormwood," said Antrobus gravely, "is one which deserves thought."

He spoke in his usual portentous way, but I could see that he was genuinely troubled.

"It is worth reflecting on," he went on, "since it illustrates my contention that nobody really knows what anybody else is thinking. Wormwood was cultural attaché in Helsinki, and we were all terrified of him. He was a lean, leathery, saturnine sort of chap with a goatee and he'd written a couple of novels of an obscurity so overwhelming as to give us an awful inferiority complex in the Chancery.

"He never spoke.

"He carried this utter speechlessness to such lengths as to be almost beyond the bounds of decency. The whole Corps quailed before him. One slow stare through those pebble-giglamps of his was enough to quell even the vivid and charming Madame Abreyville who was noted for her cleverness in bringing out the shy. She made the mistake of trying to bring Wormwood out. He stared at her hard. She was covered in confusion and trembled from head to foot. After this defeat, we all used to take cover when we saw him coming.

"One winter just before he was posted to Prague, I ran into him at a party, and finding myself wedged in behind the piano with no hope of escape, cleared my throat (I had had three Martinis) and said with what I hoped was offensive jocularity: 'What does a novelist think about at parties like these?'

"Wormwood stared at me for so long that I began to swallow my Adam's Apple over and over again as I always do when I am out of countenance. I was just about to step out of the window into a flower-bed and come round by the front door when he . . . actually spoke to me: 'Do you know what I am doing?' he said in a low hissing tone full of malevolence.

" 'No,' I said.

" 'I am playing a little game in my mind,' he said, and his expression was one of utter, murderous grimness. 'I am imagining that I am in a sleigh with the whole Diplomatic Corps. We are rushing across the Steppes, pursued by wolves. It is necessary, as they keep gaining on us, to throw a diplomat overboard from time to time in order to let the horses regain their advantage. Who would you throw first . . . and then second . . . and then third. . . ? Just look around you.'

"His tone was so alarming, so ferocious and peremptory, that I was startled; more to humour him than anything else, I said 'Madame Ventura'. She was rather a heavily-built morsel of ambassadress, eminently suitable for wolfish consumption. He curled his lip. 'She's gone already,' he said in a low, hoarse tone, glowering. 'The whole Italian mission has gone—brats included.'

"I did not quite know what to say.

" 'Er, how about our own Chancery?' I asked nervously.

" 'Oh! They've gone long ago,' he said with slow contempt, 'they've been gobbled up—including you.' He gave a yellowish shelf of rat-like teeth a half-second exposure, and then sheathed them again in his beard. I was feeling dashed awkward now, and found myself fingering my nose.

"I was relieved when I heard he had been posted.

"Now, old boy, come a series of strange events. The very next winter in Prague—that was the severe one of '37 when the wolf-packs came down to the suburbs—you may remember that two Chancery Guards and a cipher clerk were eaten by wolves? They were, it seems, out riding in a sleigh with the First Secretary Cultural. When I saw the press reports, something seemed to ring in my brain. Some half-forgotten memory. . . . It worried me until I went to the Foreign Office List and looked up the Prague Mission. It was Wormwood. It gave me food for deep thought.

"But time passed, and for nearly ten years I heard no more of Wormwood. Then came that report of wolves eating the Italian Ambassador on the Trieste-Zagreb road in mid-winter. You remember the case? The victim was in a car this time. I do not have to tell you who was driving. Wormwood.

"Then once again a long period of time passed without any news of him. But yesterday" . . . Antrobus' voice trembled at this point in the narrative and he drew heavily on his cigar.

"Yesterday, I had a long letter from Bunty Scott-

Peverel who is Head of Chancery in Moscow. There is a passage in it which I will read to you. Here it is. . . .

" 'We have just got a new Cultural Sec., rather an odd sort of fellow, a writer I believe. Huge fronded beard, pebble specs and glum as all highbrows are. He has taken a *dumka* about twenty miles outside Moscow where he intends to entertain in some style. Usually these hunting lodges are only open in the summer. But he intends to travel by *droshky* and is busy getting one built big enough, he says, to accommodate the whole Dip. Corps which he will invite to his housewarming. It is rather an original idea, and we are all looking forward to it very much and waiting impatiently for this giant among *droshkies* to be finished.'

"You will understand," said Antrobus, "the thrill of horror with which I read this letter. I have written at length to Bunty, setting out my fears. I hope I shall be in time to avert what might easily become the first wholesale pogrom in the history of diplomacy. I hope he heeds my words. But I am worried, I confess. I scan the papers uneasily every morning. Is that the *Telegraph*, by any chance, protruding from the pocket of your mackintosh?"

A recital of national poetry by the
Dutch Ambassadress.

8

La Valise

"If there is anything worse than a soprano," said Antrobus judicially as we walked down the Mall towards his
club, "it is a mezzo-soprano. One shriek lower in the
scale, perhaps, but with higher candle-power. I'm not
just being small-minded, old chap. I bear the scars of
spiritual experience. Seriously." And indeed he did look
serious; but then he always does. The aura of the Foreign
Office clings to him. He waved his umbrella, changed
step, and continued in a lower, more confidential register.
"And I can tell you another thing. If there is anything
really questionable about the French character it must be
its passion for *culture*. I might not dare to say this in the
F.O. old man, but I know you will respect my confidence.
You see, we are all supposed to be pro rather than anti in
the Old Firm—but as for me, frankly I hate the stuff. It
rattles me. It gives me the plain untitivated pip, I don't
mind confessing."

He drew a deep breath and after a pause went on, more
pensively, drawing upon his memories of Foreign Service

life: "All my worst moments have been cultural rather than political. Like that awful business of *La Valise*, known privately to the members of the Corps as The Diplomatic Bag Extraordinary. Did I ever mention it? She was French Ambassadress in Vulgaria."

"No."

"Shall I? It will make you wince."

"Do."

"Well it happened while I was serving in Vulgaria some years ago; an unspeakable place full of unspeakable people. It was the usual Iron Curtain post to which the F.O. had exposed its soft white underbelly in the person of Smith-Cromwell. Not that he was a bad chap. He was in fact quite intelligent and had played darts for Cambridge. But he was easily led. As you know in a Communist country the Corps finds itself cut off from every human contact. It has to provide its own amusements, fall back on its own resources. And this is where the trouble usually begins. It is a strange thing but in a post like that it is never long before some dastardly Frenchman (always French) reaches for the safety-catch of his revolver and starts to introduce *culture* into our lives. Invariably.

"So it fell out with us in Sczbog. Sure enough, during my second winter the French appointed a Cultural Attaché, straight from Montmartre—the place with the big church. Fellow like a greyhound. Burning eyes. Dirty hair. A moist and Fahrenheit handshake. You know the type. Wasn't even married to his own wife. Most Questionable fellow. Up till now everything had been quiet and reasonable—just the usual round of diplomatic-social engagements among colleagues. Now this beastly fellow started the ball rolling with a public lecture—an undisguised public lecture—on a French writer called, if I understood him correctly, Flowbear. Of course we all had to go to support the French. Cultural reciprocity and all that. But as if this wasn't enough the little blackhead followed it up with another about another blasted French writer called, unless my memory is at fault, Goaty-eh. I ask you, my dear fellow, what was one to do. Flowbear! Goaty-eh! It was more than flesh and blood could stand. I myself feared the worst as I sat listening to him. The whole thing cried out for the chloroform-pad. I had of course wound up and set my features at Refined Rapture like everyone else, but inside me I was in a turmoil of apprehension. Culture spreads like mumps, you know, like measles. A thing like this could get everyone acting unnaturally in no time. All culture corrupts, old boy, but French culture corrupts absolutely. I was not wrong.

"The echoes had hardly died away when I noticed That Awful Look coming over peoples' faces. Everyone began to think up little tortures of their own. A whole winter stretched before us with practically no engagements except a national day or so. It was clear that unless Smith-Cromwell took a strong line the rot would set in. He did not. Instead of snorting when *La Valise* embarked on a cultural season he weakly encouraged her; he was even heard to remark that culture was a Good Thing— for the Military Attaché.

"At this time of course we also had our cultural man. Name of Gool. And he looked it. It was a clear case of Harrow and a bad third in History. But up to now we had kept Gool strictly under control and afraid to move. It could not last. He was bound to come adrift. Within a month he was making common cause with his French colleague. They began to lecture, separately and together.

73

They gave readings with writhings. They spared us nothing, Eliot, Sartre, Emmanuel Kant—and who is that other fellow? The name escapes me. In short they gave us everything short of Mrs. Beeton. I did my best to get an arm-lock on Gool and to a certain extent succeeded by threatening to recommend him for an O.B.E. He knew this would ruin his career and that he would be posted to Java. But by the time I had got him pressed to the mat it was too late. The whole Corps had taken fire and was burning with the old hard gem-like flame. Culture was spreading like wildfire.

"A series of unforgettable evenings now began, old boy. Each mission thought up some particularly horrible contribution of its own to this feast. The nights became a torture of pure poesy and song. An evening of hellish amateur opera by the Italians would be followed without intermission by an ear-splitting evening of yodelling from the Swiss, all dressed as edelweiss. Then the Japanese mission went beserk and gave a Noh-play of ghoulish obscurity lasting seven hours. The sight of all those little yellowish, inscrutable diplomats all dressed as Mickey Mouse, old boy, was enough to turn milk. And their voices simply ate into one. Then in characteristic fashion the Dutch, not to be outdone, decided to gnaw their way to the forefront of things with a recital of national poetry by the Dutch Ambassadress herself. This was when I began to draft my resignation in my own mind. O God! how can I ever forget Madame Vanderpipf (usually the most kind and normal of wives and mothers) taking up a stance like a grenadier at Fontenoy, and after a pause declaiming in a slow, deep—O unspeakably slow and deep—voice, the opening verses of whatever it was? Old Boy, the cultural heritage of the Dutch is not my

74

affair. Let them have it, I say. Let them enjoy it peacefully as they may. But spare me from poems of five hundred lines beginning, '*Oom kroop der poop*'. You smile, as well indeed you may, never having heard Mrs. Vanderpipf declaiming those memorable stanzas with all the sullen fire of her race. Listen!

> *Oom kroop der poop*
> *Zoom kroon der soup*
> *Soon droon der oopersnoop.*

"And so on. Have you got the idea? Perhaps there is something behind it all—who am I to say? All I know is that it is no joke to be on the receiving end. Specially as she would pause from time to time to give a rough translation in pidgin for Smith-Cromwell's benefit. Something like this: 'Our national poet Snugerpouf, he says eef Holland lives forever, only, how you would say?, heroes from ze soil oopspringing, yes?' It was pulse-stopping, old man. Then she would take a deep breath and begin afresh.

> *Oom kroop der poop*
> *Zoom kroon der soup.*

"In after years the very memory of this recitation used to make the sweat start out of my forehead. You must try it for yourself sometime. Just try repeating '*oom kroop der poop*' five hundred times in a low voice. After a time it's like Yoga. Everything goes dark. You feel you are falling backwards into illimitable black space.

"By this time Smith-Cromwell himself had begun to suffer. He leaned across to me once on this particular evening to whisper a message. I could tell from his popping eye and the knot of throbbing veins at his temple

75

that he was under strain. He had at last discovered what culture means. 'If this goes on much longer,' he hissed, 'I shall confess everything.'

"But this did go on; unremittingly for a whole winter. I spare you a description of the cultural offerings brought to us by the remoter tribes. The Argentines! The Liberians! Dear God! When I think of the Chinese all dressed in lamp-shades, the Australians doing sheep-opera, the Egyptians undulating and ululating all in the same breath. . . . Old boy I am at a loss.

"But the real evil demon of the peace was *La Valise*. Whenever culture flagged she was there, quick to rekindle the flame. Long after the Corps was milked dry, so to speak, and had nothing left in its collective memory except nursery rhymes or perhaps a bluish limerick or two, *La Valise* was still at it. She fancied herself as a singer. She was never without a wad of music. A mezzo soprano never gives in, old boy. She dies standing up, with swelling port curved to the stars. . . . And here came this beastly attaché again. He had turned out to be a pianist, and she took him everywhere to accompany her. While he clawed the piano she clawed the air and remorselessly sang. How she sang! Always a bit flat, I gather, but with a sickening lucid resonance that penetrated the middle ear. Those who had hearing-aids filled them with a kapok mixture for her recitals. When she hit a top note I could hear the studs vibrating in my dinner-shirt. Cowed, we sat and watched her, as she started to climb a row of notes towards the veil of the temple—that shattering top E, F or G: I never know which. We had the sinking feeling you get on the giant racer just as it nears the top of the slope. To this day I don't know how we kept our heads.

"Smith-Cromwell was by this time deeply penitent

about his earlier encouragement of *La Valise* and at his
wits' end to see her stopped. Everyone in the Chancery
was in a bad state of nerves. The Naval Attaché had taken
to bursting into tears at meals if one so much as men-
tioned a forthcoming cultural engagement. But what was to
be done? We clutched at every straw; and De Mandeville,
always resourceful, suggested inviting the Corps to a live
reading by himself and chauffeur from the works of the
Marquis De Sade. But after deliberation Smith-Cromwell
thought this might, though Effective, seem Questionable,
so we dropped it.

"I had begun to feel like Titus Andronicus, old man,
when the miracle happened. Out of a cloudless sky.
Nemesis intervened just as he does in Gilbert Murray.
Now *La Valise* had always been somewhat hirsute, indeed quite distinctly moustached in the Neapolitan
manner, though none of us for a moment suspected the
truth. But one day after Christmas M. De Panier, her hus-
band, came round to the Embassy in full *tenue* and threw
himself into Cromwell-Smith's arms, bathed in tears as
the French always say. 'My dear Britannic Colleague,' he
said, 'I have come to take my leave of you. My career is
completely ruined. I am leaving diplomacy for good. I
have resigned. I shall return to my father-in-law's carpet-
factory near Lyons and start a new life. All is over.'

"Smith-Cromwell was of course delighted to see the
back of *La Valise*; but we all had a soft corner for De
Panier. He was a gentleman. Never scamped his *frais* and
always gave us real champagne on Bastille Day. Also his
dinners were dinners—not like the Swedes; but I am
straying from my point. In answer to Smith-Cromwell's
tactful inquiries De Panier unbosomed.

"You will never credit it, old man. You will think I am

romancing. But it's as true as I am standing here. There are times in life when the heart spires upward like the lark on the wing; when through the consciousness runs, like an unearthly melody, the thought that God *really* exists, really *cares*; more, that he turns aside to lend a helping hand to poor dips *in extremis*. This was such a moment, old boy.

"*La Valise* had gone into hospital for some minor complaint which defied diagnosis. And in the course of a minor operation the doctors discovered that she was *turning into a man!* Nowadays of course it is becoming a commonplace of medicine; but at the time of which I speak it sounded like a miracle. A *man*, upon my soul! We could hardly believe it. The old caterpillar was really one of *us*. It was too enchanting! We were saved!

"And so it turned out. Within a matter of months her voice—that instrument of stark doom—sank to a bass; she sprouted a beard. Poor old De Panier hastened to leave but was held up until his replacement came. Poor fellow! Our hearts went out to him with This Whiskered Wonder on his hands. But he took it all very gallantly. They left at last, in a closed car, at dead of night. He would be happier in Lyons, I reflected, where nobody minds that sort of thing.

"But if he was gallant about this misfortune so was *La Valise elle-même*. She went on the halls, old boy, as a bass-baritone and made quite a name for herself. Smith-Cromwell says he once heard her sing 'The London Derrière' in Paris with full orchestra and that she brought the house down. Some of the lower notes still made the ash-trays vibrate a bit but it was no longer like being trapped in a wind-tunnel. She wore a beard now and a corkscrew moustache and was very self-possessed. One can afford to be Over There. He also noticed she was wearing a smartish pair of elastic-sided boots. O, and her trade name now was Tito Torez. She and De Panier were divorced by then, and she had started out on a new career which was less of a reign of terror, if we can trust Smith-Cromwell. Merciful are the ways of Providence!

"As for poor De Panier himself, I gather that he re-entered the service after the scandal had died down. He is at present Consul-General in Blue Springs, Colorado. I'm told that there isn't much culture there, so he ought to be a very happy man indeed."

The Thumb . . . was an iron one

9

The Iron Hand

Have you ever noticed (said Antrobus) that people called Percy are almost invariably imbeciles? Perhaps the name confers a fateful instability upon the poor souls; perhaps it is chosen as the most appropriate for those who, from birth, show all the signs of being lathe-turned morons. . . . Anyway it is a fact. Hearing the name I know I need never look at the face. I am sure of the ears spread to the four winds like banana-leaves, sure of the lustreless eyes, the drooling mouth, hammer-toes and so on . . . Percy is as Percy looks in my experience.

Nor was Percy, the Embassy second-footman, any exception. In fact to call him a footman was an insult to what is, after all, a *métier*. He was a superannuated pot-boy with the sort of face one sees slinking out of cinemas in places like Sidcup and Penge—idle, oafish and conceited. He spent hours tending the spitcurl on his receding forehead and complacently ogling the housemaids. He rode a bicycle round and round the flower-beds until Polk-Mowbray (bird-watching from his office) became giddy and ordered him to desist. He whistled with a dreadful monotonous shrillness. He chewed gum with a sickening rotary action that turned the beholder's stomach.

Well, when Drage went on leave the domestic arrangements of the Embassy were confided to this junior Quasimodo, and that is how the business of the iron hand came about. Normally Percy was never allowed to touch either the Embassy plate or the suit of armour which stood in the Conference Room and which we used to call "The White Knight". Personally I hated the thing, though Drage loved it dearly. It was always giving us frights during Secret Conferences. Once the beaver came down with a clang just as Polk-Mowbray was about to Come To A Decision and we all got a dreadful start. On another occasion smoke was seen curling out of its mouth and the cry of "Spy" went up from one and all. Trampelvis had dropped a cigar-end into it. After this I had it moved into the hall. Once a month Drage used to take it apart and polish it up. Now Percy had his glaucous eye fixed firmly upon "The White Knight", and no sooner had Drage left than he at once began to fool around with the thing.

He put the headpiece on and scared the housemaids by gargling at them through the buttery hatch after dark. He even went for a twilight ride on his bicycle dressed in the thing—out of one gate and in at the other—which made the startled Vulgarian sentries rub their eyes. Why they didn't shoot him I don't know. It must have seemed clear evidence that the Secret Service was going over on to the offensive—and one little arpeggio on a sub-machine gun would have saved us so much subsequent trouble. . . .

THE IRON HAND

Well, these benighted pranks went on until one day Percy met his Waterloo. After a successful appearance as Hamlet's father he regained the buttery one day, panting happily, and started to divest himself of helm and codpiece in time to serve a pre-dinner Martini in the sitting-room. Judge the poor mawk's surprise when he found that the right hand wouldn't unscrew according to plan. All the wrenching and pulling in the world could not budge it. In a flash he realized that unless he cut along the dotted line this grotesque mailed fist was with him for life. The press-stud or what-have-you was jammed against the demi-quiver of the bassinet, more or less. The first I heard of it was a noise which suggested that someone was trying to shoe a mettlesome carthorse in the Residence— rustic, yet somehow out of keeping with Polk-Mowbray's ways. It didn't seem natural. It didn't fit into Our World. Listening more carefully I thought I heard the sound of human groans, and I was not wrong. The cry for a certified obstetrician had already been raised.

Percy was sobbing like a donkey, surrounded by frightened housemaids. He realized that he was dished. There he sat on the three-legged stool in the buttery, bathed in tears, and holding up this expensive-looking piece of ironmongery in dumb appeal. "Wretched oaf!" I cried. "You have been told a hundred times not to touch 'The White Knight'." I pulled and tugged, but it was no go; the iron boxing-glove was stuck clean as a cavalry boot. Various fruitless suggestions were made, various attempts to divest him were carried out. In vain. I took him into the Chancery in search of qualified advice. Spalding tried, De Mandeville tried. We pushed and pulled and heaved in unison. Percy sobbed more loudly. But the thing refused to yield. Polk-Mowbray and a couple of archivists made their appearance, intrigued by the noises from a normally sedate Chancery. They brought fresh blood and fresh impetus to his rescuers. While Polk-Mowbray stood on his chest we formed a human chain—like getting the Lowestoft Lifeboat in— and tried to wrest the article from him by brute force. It was no go. A little more and we should have shredded Frederick. A private socket would have given. "There's no need to yell so," said Spalding angrily. "We are only trying to help you." We desisted panting and had another conference. Dovebasket summoned the Embassy chauffeurs and took counsel with them. Now plans were formulated involving expensive and bizarre equipment— for they planned to saw their way in with a hacksaw and so deliver the lad. But they punctured him. Then Polk-Mowbray boldly tried to hammer the thing off with a croquet mallet. The noise was deafening, the result nil. I must say those medieval farriers, artificers—or whatever they were called—knew their business. It didn't look much, this olde worlde gauntlet, but heavens how it stuck. Percy was by now very much frightened and perhaps slightly bruised around the edges. We plied him with bonded gin to bring the roses back. There he sat in Spalding's swivel-chair, letting out a moan from time to time, and drinking thirstily. Occasionally one of us would have a new idea and advance upon him, whereupon he would swivel wildly in order to avoid further pain. In this way he dealt Butch Benbow a backhand stroke with his glove across the shoulders which felled our redoubtable Naval Attaché and kept him down for the count. More gin, more moans. There seemed to be no way out of the *impasse*. Time was running out. Guests were expected. "I've a good mind to dress you up in the rest of

this thing and send you back to your mother by air!"
cried Polk-Mowbray in a transport of fury. I felt for him.

The awful thing was that the Dutch were due to dine
with us that evening. It always seemed to be the fate of
the Dutch to be invited on crisis evenings. That evening
was a real *kermesse héroique*. Percy was a poor butler at the
best of times but tonight he bordered on the really
original. He shambled round and round the room sniffing,
half anaesthetized by gin and . . . well, you can imagine
our guests' faces when a mailed hand appeared over their
shoulder holding a soup-plate. They *must* have felt that
there was something uncanny about it. Clearly they
longed to pop a question but the Iron Laws of the Corps
forbade it. They held their curiosity in leash. They were
superb. Normally Percy always got his thumb in the soup
—but the thumb this evening was an iron one. I shudder
to recall it. Yet by a superhuman effort we remained
calm and Talked Policy as coolly as we could. The old
training dies hard. Somehow we managed to carry it off.
Yet I think our hosts felt themselves to be in the presence
of irremediable tragedy. They pressed our hands in silent
sympathy as we tucked them into their cars. All of a
sudden one felt terribly alone again—alone with the Iron
Hand. . . .

Well, my dear fellow, everyone had a go at that blasted
hand—the Chaplain, the cipher staff, finally the doctor.
The latter wanted to heat the whole thing up with a blow-
torch until the press-stud expanded but that would have
incinerated Percy. By this time, of course, I hardly cared
what they did to him. I would willingly have amputated
the arm from somewhere just above the waist, myself.
But meanwhile an urgent appeal had gone out to the
Museum for a professor of armour to advise us; but the

only available specialist in chain-mail was away in Italy on leave. He would not return for another two days. Two days! I know that it doesn't sound a great deal. But in the middle of the night Percy found that he had lost all trace of feeling in the arm. It had got pins and needles. He sat up in bed, haunted by a new terror. It seemed to him that gangrene had perhaps set in; he had heard the doctor muttering something about the circulation of the blood. . . . He bounded down the stairs into the Residence roaring like a lion and galloped into Polk-Mowbray's bedroom waving the object. Our esteemed Chief Of Mission, after the nervous strain of that evening, had turned in early, and was enjoying a spell of blameless slumber. Awakened by this apparition, and being unable to understand a word of Percy's gibberish, he jumped to the purely intuitive conclusion that a fire had broken out upstairs. It was a matter of moments to break glass and press button. Woken by that fateful ringing the Embassy fire squads swept gallantly into life, headed by Morgan and Chowder, pyjama-clad and in steel helmets. Just how Percy and his Ambassador escaped a thorough foam-bath that night is a mystery to me. Neither seemed very coherent to the gallant little band of rescuers as they swept through the dining-room with their sprinklers and up the stairs.

At last order was restored and the doctor summoned, who did much to soothe Percy's fears. But he did on the other hand take a serious view of the pins and needles. The circulation was being impeded by the gauntlet apparently. Percy must somehow keep the blood flowing in it—keep the circulation going—until help from the outer world arrived. How? By banging it, if you please, banging it repeatedly on anything that was to hand, banging it day and night lest the gangrene set in. I tell you, my dear chap, that that fateful banging, which lasted two whole days and nights, rings in my ears even now. Banging on the walls, the buttery table, on the floor. Neither work nor sleep was possible. An army of poltergeists could not have done half as well. Bang, bang, bang . . . now loud and slow, now hollow and resonant, now sharp and clear. Day and night the banging haunted us until at last the Professor appeared. We received him with tears of entreaty in our eyes.

He took a look at Percy and nodded sagely. He knew, it appeared, all about these press-studs. He applied some olive-oil on a feather to the relevant joints, tapped twice with his pince-nez and Presto: Percy was free. It seemed almost too good to be true—all that silence. A united sigh went up from us all—a sigh such as I have never heard from dips before or since. Silence at last descended on us, the silence of a normal embassy oozing along at the normal cruising speed. No longer the goods' yards at Swindon, no longer a branch of Bassett-Lowke, no longer a boiler-makers' jamboree in Sheffield. No. Just H.M. Embassy as ever was, as ever would be in future, we hoped. But just to make assurance doubly sure Polk-Mowbray had the arms taken off the suit of armour and sent home. I can't say it improved the appearance of "The White Knight"; but then it was questionable whether anything ever could.

10

The Swami's Secret

I told you (said Antrobus) about the Naval Attaché and
his definite leanings towards the occult? I thought I had.
I don't think, however, that I ever told you about the
business of the Swami. Well, the whole of my first winter
old Butch Benbow, as he was laughingly called, was
working away like hell on reincarnation. Breathing exer-
cises in this office, squinting at the tip of his tongue for
hours at a time until his P.A. nearly went out of her mind.
He even took to holding his breath during the duller staff
conferences and letting it out with a swish. This wasn't
reassuring. His valet said that during the lunch interval
he often sat cross-legged on the lawn with a begonia on
his navel, frankly and openly meditating—but this may
have been an exaggeration. Anyway, he had it bad, and
he was nothing if not dogged. Indeed doggedness was
clearly marked in his horoscope, he said. There was no
mention of drunkenness or indecent exposure. Just the
doggedness. Mind you, I myself doubted the wisdom of
all this spiritual strain upon a nature which, I thought,
was of a more spirituous cast, but . . . I held my

peace. Even when he sprained a rib I said nothing.

Then one morning he came into my office and I was staggered by the change in his appearance. He walked like an aged and broken man. He was ashen pale. At first I put this down to the fact that we had all dined at the Burmese Legation the night before where they had served venison so rare as almost to lift one off the ground. But I was wrong. "Antrobus," he said, "I'm ruined, old man. Dished. My blasted swami is coming out by air."

"Your swami?" I echoed. He nodded and gulped.

"I've been taking reincarnation lessons by post from an Indian swami. Up to now he's simply been a Box Number in the Edgware Road, old man. Name of Anaconda Veranda. And jolly fruitful it's been up to now. But I wasn't prepared for a telegram saying that he was coming out to visit me and study my spiritual progress at first hand. He is arriving this afternoon."

"Well what's wrong with that?" I said, looking for the Silver Lining. "I bet you are the first dip. to have a private swami. Everyone will be mad with envy in the Corps." He groaned and moved from side to side, as if he were representing Colic in a charade. He said:

"My dear chap, surely you know that all swamis are little naked men in spectacles walking around with a goat on a string? What could I do with him here? I couldn't take him to cocktails with the French. I should become the laughing-stock of the whole Corps if I were seen bowling about attached to a man in a loin-cloth. The press would certainly get hold of it. What would the Admiralty say if they saw a picture of me in the Navy Weekly? You know how materialistic they are. It would mean the China Station again, and my liver wouldn't stand it."

THE SWAMI'S SECRET

I took a deep breath. I began to see his point. A loin-cloth is a tricky thing in diplomacy; in the hands of the Ill-Disposed it could become a Secret Weapon. I pondered.

"Well," I said at last, "you will have to try and Carry It Off somehow. Pretend he's a cousin of somebody important like Noel Coward or Bruce Lockhart. It's the only chance." But he was sunk in gloom and hardly heeded me. "And then there's another thing," he said gloomily. "I'm supposed to be living on goat's milk—not unsweetened condensed touched up with Gordon's Dry. Somehow I couldn't bring myself to keep a goat in the house. They smell so. I expect he'll give me a dressing down on spiritual grounds when he finds out. And honestly, Antrobus, I don't see myself passing him off as a relation, do you?" To be honest I didn't really; but what was to be done? The plane had already left London with Butch's little spiritual adviser aboard. We would have to face up to reality. I confess my heart ached for old Butch.

But if he was pale now, my colleague, he was a great deal paler that afternoon as he got into the official car and set off for the airport to meet his swami. I didn't blame him. The dew of death had settled on his somewhat receding brow. The poor chap could see himself socially dished as well spiritually pooped.

Imagine his relief, however, when out of the aircraft stepped—not a naked Dravidian leading a quarantined goat—but the most poised and charming of Indian princelings, clad in beautifully cut clothes and wearing a turban with an emerald the size of a goitre in it. Anaconda Veranda was perfectly delightful, a Man Of The World, a Gentleman. Butch nearly fainted with relief as he

listened to his perfect English, his exquisite English—
rather better than Butch's own brand of the stuff. Could
this be the swami he so much dreaded? Butch swooned
back in his car muttering prayers of thanksgiving. By the
time he reached the Embassy with his swami he was a
changed man. He was swollen with pride, gloating almost.

I must say I found Veranda—everyone found him—
perfectly delightful. It seems that he had been at Oxford
with all of us—though strangely enough nobody remembered him. But he was as unbashfully Balliol as it is possible to be. And far from receiving the acid drop Butch
found himself the most sought-after man in the Corps.
All because of his swami. Veranda danced beautifully, was
modest, wise, witty and gentle; he also played the flute to
distraction which endeared him frightfully to Polk-
Mowbray. He was even spiritually accommodating and
let Butch know that in certain stages of spiritual develop-
ment the odd touch of gin in unsweetened condensed is
just the job and has the unofficial approval of the Dalai
Lama. Butch was in ecstasies. So were we all.

Veranda did quite a bit of drawing-room occultism,
turning tables and telling fortunes until the Ladies of the
Corps were almost mad with flattery and apprehension.
He hypnotized Drage and took an endless succession of
hard-boiled eggs out of his nose. He predicted Collin's
appointment to China. He told Dovebasket the size of
his overdraft to two places of decimals. My dear chap, he
was a Man of Parts. In next to no time he had most of the
Ambassadresses pleading openly for spiritual instruction
while the Heads Of Mission, mad with envy, were cabling
their head office for swamis to be sent out on approval by
air freight. Polk-Mowbray even conceived the idea of
creating a special post of Senior Spiritual Adviser to the

Embassy and appointing Veranda to it. Just to keep him with us. But I think the Chaplain intervened and quashed the idea. Polk-Mowbray sulked a good deal after this.

Well, for a whole season Veranda occupied the social spotlight, to our intense pride. He dined here, he dined there. He was put up for the O.B.E. and the Croix De Guerre—and quite a lot of other decorations. As a social draw he was unequalled, a human magnet. And of course Butch went up to the top of the class. He had to engage a private secretary to keep his now bulging Engagements Book and head off mere climbers with the Retort Civil (but Cutting). He was a happy man.

But now comes the *dénouement*—which poor Polk-Mowbray probably refers to as "the pay-off" nowadays. It happened quite suddenly and gracefully. I must say that Veranda must have made a close social study of the Corps and its movements. He chose one of those ghastly holidays—was it Labour Day?—when he could be sure that the whole Corps was sitting on a dais in the main square of the town, perspiring freely and watching the infantry defile—if that is the word. Yes, it was beautifully conceived, perfectly timed. He started by borrowing the official car and a dozen of De Mandeville's pigskin suit-cases. In leisurely fashion, and with that irresistibly endearing smile which had won so many friends and influenced so many people—he made a tour of the Embassies cleaning them out with judgement and discretion. Such selectivity, old man. Only the best seemed to be good enough. Just the top jewellery like Polk-Mowbray's dress studs, Angela's tiara . . . the top treasures like the original Leonardo drawings in the Argentine Legation, the two Tiepolos *chez* the Italians, the first edition of Hamlet in Spalding's library, the two Mycenaean brooches of the Greek Ambassadress. He even took Nelson's Dress Sword which was Butch's only real treasure and on which he always made toast in the winter. And with all this stuff safely stowed in his saddle-bags the fellow evaporated, snuffed himself out, dematerialized.... Well, old boy, you can imagine the rumpus. What an eruption! At first one hardly believed it. Surprised! You could have sluiced us down with frangipani. Many was the hanging head, many the pallid glance. Poor Butch found himself at the bottom of the form again—so did we all. For this terrible house-guest had become firmly identified with our Mission. I don't know how we lived through the next few months. Butch's swami was never traced, nor was any single item from all this cultural boodle. Somewhere among the bazaars of India these treasures must be on sale. One blenches to think of it.

It took Butch years to live down his swami. But the worst of it all was that he never finished his reincarnation course; somehow he hadn't the heart to go on. Nor has he ever had the heart or the social courage to try another swami. And as he hasn't mastered the drill he lives—so I understand from common friends—in perpetual terror of being reincarnated as a soldier.